NATIVITY

cynthia rylant

BEACH LANE BOOKS

New York London Toronto Sydney New Delhi

And there were shepherds
abiding in the field, keeping watch
over their flock by night.

And, lo,
the angel of the Lord came upon them.

The angel said,
   Fear not, for behold, I bring you good tidings
   of great joy. For unto you this day is born
   a savior. And this shall be a sign to you:
   you will find the babe lying in a manger.

Then suddenly there was with the angel
a multitude of angels, saying Glory to God,
and on earth peace, good will toward men.

And the shepherds came unto Bethlehem
and found Mary, with her husband, Joseph,
and the babe, who was lying in a manger.

The shepherds made known to others the saying which was told them about the child.

And all they that heard this story wondered at those things which were told them.

But Mary kept these things
and pondered them in her heart.

When the babe, who was called Jesus,
became a man, he stood one day on a
mountain before a great multitude of people.
And he said:

Blessed are the poor,

for theirs is the kingdom of heaven.

Blessed are they that mourn,
for they shall be comforted.

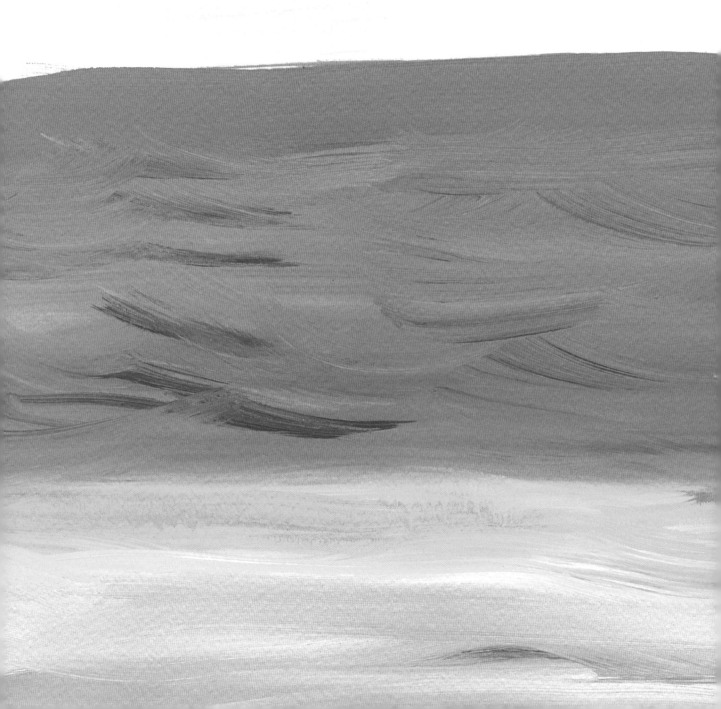

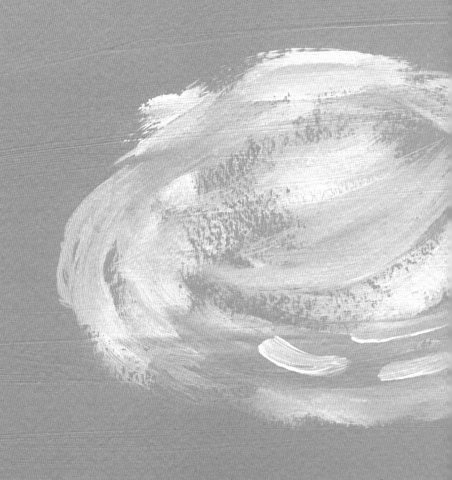

Blessed are the meek,

for they shall inherit the earth.

Blessed are the pure in heart . . .

for they shall see God.

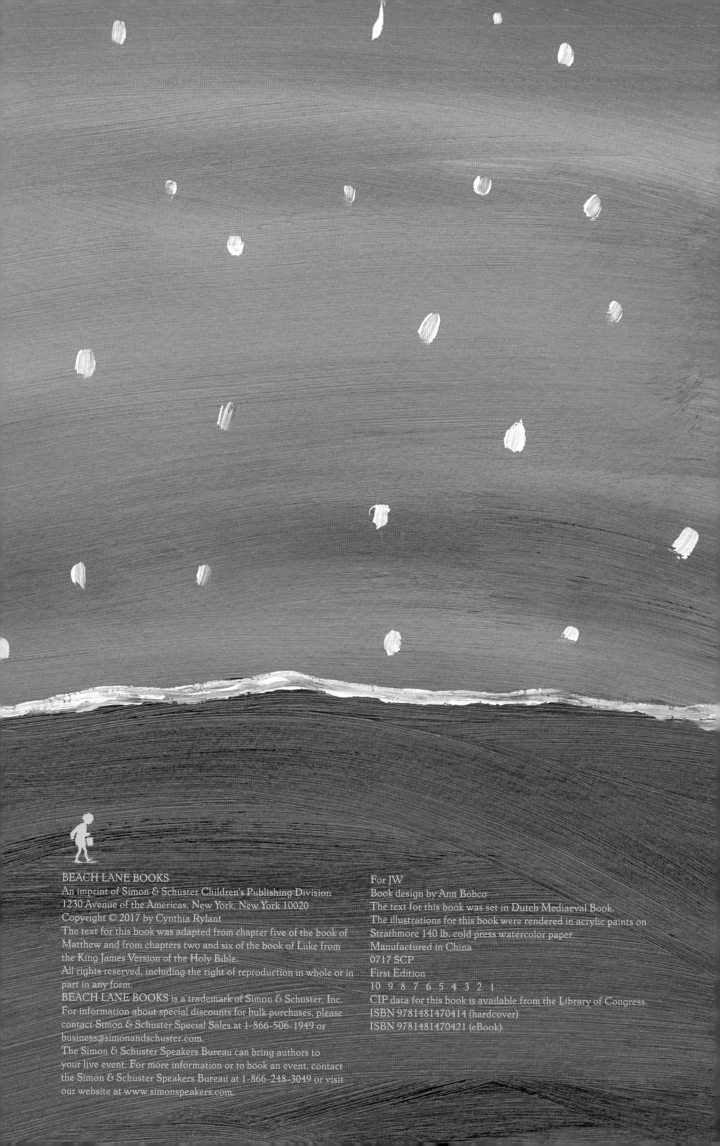

BEACH LANE BOOKS
An imprint of Simon & Schuster Children's Publishing Division
1230 Avenue of the Americas, New York, New York 10020
Copyright © 2017 by Cynthia Rylant
The text for this book was adapted from chapter five of the book of
Matthew and from chapters two and six of the book of Luke from
the King James Version of the Holy Bible.
All rights reserved, including the right of reproduction in whole or in
part in any form.
BEACH LANE BOOKS is a trademark of Simon & Schuster, Inc.
For information about special discounts for bulk purchases, please
contact Simon & Schuster Special Sales at 1-866-506-1949 or
business@simonandschuster.com.
The Simon & Schuster Speakers Bureau can bring authors to
your live event. For more information or to book an event, contact
the Simon & Schuster Speakers Bureau at 1-866-248-3049 or visit
our website at www.simonspeakers.com.

For JW
Book design by Ann Bobco
The text for this book was set in Dutch Mediaeval Book.
The illustrations for this book were rendered in acrylic paints on
Strathmore 140 lb. cold press watercolor paper.
Manufactured in China
0717 SCP
First Edition
10 9 8 7 6 5 4 3 2 1
CIP data for this book is available from the Library of Congress.
ISBN 9781481470414 (hardcover)
ISBN 9781481470421 (eBook)